Archway Publishing books may be ordered through booksellers or by contacting:

Archway Publishing
1663 Liberty Drive
Bloomington, IN 47403
www.archwaypublishing.com
1 (888) 242-5904

Because of the dynamic nature of the Internet, any web addresses or links contained in this book may have changed since publication and may no longer be valid. The views expressed in this work are solely those of the author and do not necessarily reflect the views of the publisher, and the publisher hereby disclaims any responsibility for them.

Any people depicted in stock imagery provided by Thinkstock are models, and such images are being used for illustrative purposes only. Certain stock imagery © Thinkstock.

ISBN: 978-1-4808-3232-9 (sc)
ISBN: 978-1-4808-3233-6 (hc)
ISBN: 978-1-4808-3231-2 (e)

Print information available on the last page.

Archway Publishing rev. date: 09/26/2016

Dedication:

"For Josie"

With abundant thanks to my family, EG, and my talented illustrator, Anne Saxelby.

It all began when Mom and Dad bought a new apartment. They said our family needed more space because Josie the Great was coming!

Max and Bear wondered...

Who's Josie the Great?

The new apartment was in a big, tall, building in Brooklyn. On top of the building it said "COOP". Max and Bear saw a sign like that at the zoo.

Max and Bear wondered... Would they be living with chickens? There were chickens living under that sign at the Prospect Park Zoo.

Could Josie the Great be a chicken? A pet chicken would be great!

Movers came to the old apartment, packed everything in big, brown, bulging boxes, and loaded them onto a huge truck.

Max and Bear wondered...

Would they get packed in a big brown box on the huge truck too?

Could Josie the Great be in a box?

t the new apartment there was a lovely lobby, lacking chickens, and a man called a doorman.

Max and Bear wondered...

Could a man be made of doors?

The Doorman, actually a man in a blue suit with big brass buttons, opened doors! He opened the elevator door that whisked them up to their new apartment.

Once inside Max and Bear began exploring. They were quite surprised when they spied piles of baby supplies!

Max and Bear wondered...

Mom's belly was getting big, it was hard to sit on her lap and there was a lot of talk about how great Josie was.

Who is this Josie the Great?

Then Grammy and Papa came to town, and they had a suitcase with them!

Was Josie the Great in there?

Nope!

Now Max and Bear really, really wondered...

WHERE is this Josie the Great?

The next morning, when Max and Bear woke up, Mom and Dad were gone! Suddenly Grammy's phone began bouncing, buzzing, and beeping!

Dad was calling from the hospital. "Max", Dad exclaimed, "Baby Josie is here!"

JOSIE THE GREAT IS A BABY?

Grammy and Papa took Max and Bear to the Hospital.

On their way to Mom's room, they walked past a huge glass door. Behind it, there were babies galore in little, bitty, baby bins.

Max and Bear wondered....

Was Josie the Great in one of those baby bins? Is this where she'd been? Could they go in?

Papa said, "Not yet buddy. We can't go in, so let's go see Mom!"

Max rolled his eyes and sighed. "Bear," said Max, "this Josie waiting is irritating!"

But the very next day, as Max munched a morsel of cheese from his Mama's store, Dad said, "Let's go! It's time to get Mom and Baby Jo."

At the Hospital Mom was waiting near the nurse's station, sitting in a chair with wheels, and holding a tiny bundle on her lap.

"Max", said Mom, "Come see who I have. This is your new baby sister, our little Josie the Great."

"Bear", said Max with a grin "Here's Josie the Great!"

Then he and Bear leaned in, and kissed her on her teeny, tiny, chin.

As they did, she scrunched her little nose, and heaved a great sigh, happy her big brother was standing by.

Josie the Great!

She's tiny, she's mighty, and she's here to stay!

CPSIA information can be obtained
at www.ICGtesting.com
Printed in the USA
LVOW06*1024090617

537543LV00016B/124/P

9 781480 832336